WATERSHIP DOWN

SIMON SPOTLIGHT
An imprint of Simon & Schuster Children's Publishing Division
1230 Avenue of the Americas, New York, New York 10020
This Simon Spotlight hardcover edition August 2019
First published 2018 by Macmillan Children's Books, an imprint of Pan Macmillian
20 New Wharf Road, London N1 9RR
Text and illustrations copyright © Watership Down Television Limited 2018. Watership Down © Watership Down
Television Limited 2018. Licensed by ITV Ventures.
Written by Frank Cottrell-Boyce, based on the BBC and Netflix TV miniseries script by Tom Bidwell.
Illustrations by Sophia O'Connor.
Watership Down TV miniseries based on the original story by Richard Adams.
SIMON SPOTLIGHT and colophon are registered trademarks of Simon & Schuster, Inc.
For information about special discounts for bulk purchases, please contact Simon & Schuster Special Sales at
1-866-506-1949 or business@simonandschuster.com.
Manufactured in China 0619 MCM
2 4 6 8 10 9 7 5 3 1
ISBN 978-1-5344-5706-5
ISBN 978-1-5344-5707-2 (eBook)

WATERSHIP DOWN

Retold by Frank Cottrell-Boyce
Based on the original story by Richard Adams

Simon Spotlight

New York London Toronto Sydney New Delhi

GLOSSARY

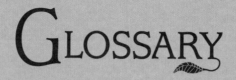

The Owsla - the strongest rabbits in a warren, who rule over the others

Hrududu - a tractor, car or other motor vehicle

Silflay - to go above ground to feed

Flay-rah - treats that wild rabbits don't usually get, such as carrots and lettuce

Elil - enemies of rabbits

Efrafa - the warren founded by General Woundwort

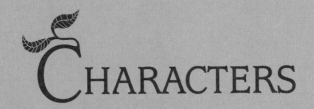

CHARACTERS

Frith
The sun-god and creator of the universe

El-ahrairah
The rabbit folk hero, smart, devious and tricky

Bigwig
Formerly a member of the Sandleford Owsla, now one of Hazel's supporters

Bluebell
A survivor of the destruction of Sandleford Warren—a natural storyteller

Threarah
Chief rabbit of the Sandleford Warren

Hazel
One of the leaders of the Sandleford rabbits

Fiver
Hazel's younger brother

Cowslip
A member of a strange warren—he invites the Sandleford rabbits to join him

Strawberry
A member of another warren, who asks to join the Sandleford rabbits

Kehaar
An injured seagull who is befriended by Hazel

General Woundwort
Chief Rabbit of Efrafa, a fearless and tyrannical leader

The Black Rabbit of Inlé
A phantom rabbit who appears when death is near

"Tell us a story, Bluebell."

"Yes, a story!"

"A new one though. One we've never heard before . . ."

At the beginning of the world, Frith, creator of the world, saw that rabbits were eating all the food.

So he gave teeth to the foxes,
and claws to the hawks and
told them to hunt the rabbits.

"Not fair!"

cried El-ahrairah—Prince of
rabbits. He persuaded Frith to
give all rabbits two gifts. First . . .

"A white tail
for warning!"

"And rabbit
trickery to help
us escape."

"Anyone with a
pair of ears knows
this old story."

"It's why El-ahrairah
is the Prince with a
Thousand Enemies."

Shush now and listen. What if there
was an enemy **crueller** than foxes?

Swifter than hawks?

More terrible than
the Black Rabbit of Inlé itself?

This is the story of how Hazel-rah and his little band defeated an elil that was greater than all the thousand enemies, and discovered a something stronger even than our Frith-given tricks and tails.

In a faraway warren called Sandleford, a **fierce** Threarah and his Owsla kept watch over all the rabbits.

But one young rabbit, Fiver, had a dream. In this dream he saw the warren covered in blood.

"It must be a warning," he said to his brother Hazel. "Some **terrible** thing is coming."

Brave Hazel went to the Threarah and said, "We must all **flee**."

"Frith in a pond!" laughed the Threarah. "Is your brother mad? What kind of fool would leave home and safety because of a dream?"

He told his Owsla to let no one leave the warren.

But Hazel believed in Fiver. That night in secret, they gathered a few friends and fled.

One member of the Owsla, a great warrior Bigwig, heard their story and decided to join them.

All night

the Owsla

hunted

them.

But they escaped from the warren and began their terrible journey. How did they travel through the pitch-dark wood?

"They followed each other's tails!"

When a conspiracy of ravens chased them for daring to enter their cathedral, how did they get away?

"Used their rabbit tricks!"

And when the Owsla chased them to the bank of a great river—the first they had ever seen—how did they get across?

"More tricks?"

They helped each other. This was their great new power.

They were not the **strongest** rabbits.

Or the **trickiest**. They were all **afraid**.

But they **believed** in each other.

"That's nice."

Sometimes Hazel thought he saw the Black Rabbit of Inlé following them, but he never told the others so they would not be scared.

They came to a great human road, where hrududu were **thundering** by.

Bigwig led them safely across.

"We're cold and hungry
and we don't know how
to dig burrows," said Bigwig.
"We should have stayed
in Sandleford."

But just then a stranger
rabbit appeared. "You can
come to our warren," he said.
"We have plenty of room.
My name is Cowslip."

Fiver was suspicious.
Rabbits never invite
strangers into their warren.

Then Cowslip said,
". . . and we have flay-rah!"

"Oh, I love flay-rah!"

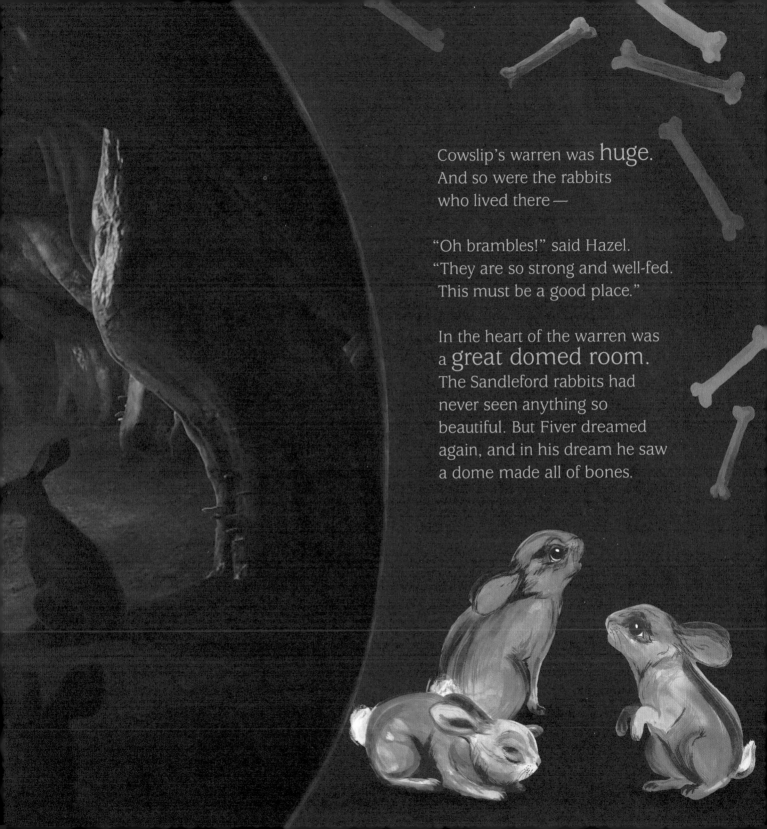

Cowslip's warren was huge.
And so were the rabbits
who lived there —

"Oh brambles!" said Hazel.
"They are so strong and well-fed.
This must be a good place."

In the heart of the warren was
a great domed room.
The Sandleford rabbits had
never seen anything so
beautiful. But Fiver dreamed
again, and in his dream he saw
a dome made all of bones.

One evening while he was out at silflay, Bigwig's neck was caught in a snare.

The stranger rabbits ran away, but Hazel and his little band managed to free Bigwig . . .

. . . and escape from Cowslip's warren.
One of the stranger rabbits ran with them.
Her name was Strawberry.

She told them how the rabbits in her warren had been
fed by the farmer for so long they had forgotten
their rabbit tricks,
their wildness,
even their stories.

"Take me with you," she said.
"I know how to dig a good burrow."

"I love a good *burrow*."

They journeyed on.

In a barn they saw a **terrible** sight—rabbits kept in cages, begging to be set free. "We want to see the sky," they cried. A dog and a cat came and chased Hazel and his band away before they could do anything.

They ran and ran until they came to a hill with a **great spreading tree.**

"Like home?"

The very same. That was
Watership Down.

The little band was not big enough to make a true warren.
Hazel decided to **rescue** the rabbits imprisoned in the barn.

This was their most **dangerous** challenge.

But as he led the prisoner-rabbits to freedom, Hazel saw that someone was following him . . .

the Black Rabbit of Inlé.

"Hazel," she called.

"I've followed you this far.

Run away now but I will catch you one day."

Up on Watership Down the rabbits had no fear. "We can see for miles," said Bigwig. "No enemy will be able to get near us."

As he said this, a shadow fell over him. A great bird crashed into the hill. The bird was hurt. They fed him and cared for him.

"But birds are elil!"

Sometimes. But Hazel and his band had learned that fear is a useful servant but a terrible master. This bird was named Kehaar.

"Like Kehaar our friend!"

This was that very same Kehaar. He was younger then. As soon as his wings were mended, he flew over the hills and told the rabbits what he had seen.

"I saw another warren—a **terrible** place, like a prison. They call it **Efrafa**. The Efrafan Owsla guard the other rabbits all the time.

Their leader knows all about your warren—he wants to **destroy** it. You little rabbits have no chance against him. They call him General Woundwort."

Bigwig went to Efrafa to see if any of the rabbits wanted to leave with him. But the Efrafan Owsla would not let him leave.

"I'm scared now!"

Then listen.

That night, when Bigwig did
not return, Fiver dreamed a
great rabbit trick.
Hazel led a group of rabbits to
the farm. They teased the farm dog.

When it chased them, they led it
into the midst of Woundwort's
forces there on Watership Down.

General Woundwort was killed.

The trick had been clever but dangerous
too. Weary and bruised, Hazel lay down.
Someone was coming toward him.

The Black Rabbit of Inlé.

But now Hazel had learned not to
be afraid. Instead of running away,
he went with the Black Rabbit.

"The rabbits of Watership Down
will be safe now," said the
Black Rabbit, "for they
have their tricks
and they have their
white tails ...

...and most of
all, they care
for each other.
So fear will never
be their master."